Hop and Run

by **Karen Wallace** and **Ailie Busby**

W

FRANKLIN WATTS
LONDON•SYDNEY

Mouse and Rabbit
went into the garden.

They wanted to play.

"Look at me,"
said Mouse.

"I can run
under the broom."

"Look at me,"
said Rabbit.

"I can hop
over the broom."

"Look at me,"
said Mouse.

"I can run
under the fence."

"Look at me,"
said Rabbit.

"I can hop
over the fence."

"Look at me,"
said Mouse.

"I can run
under the table."

Oh no!

Rabbit hit a pot.

Crash! Smash!

The pot fell down.

The boy ran
out of the house.

Rabbit hopped
over the fence.

Mouse ran
under the fence.

Story trail

Start at the beginning of the story trail. Ask your child to retell the story in their own words, pointing to each picture in turn to recall the sequence of events.

Start

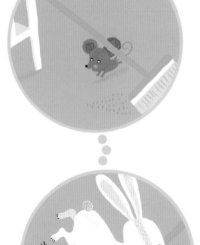

Independent Reading

This series is designed to provide an opportunity for your child to read on their own. These notes are written for you to help your child choose a book and to read it independently.

In school, your child's teacher will often be using reading books which have been banded to support the process of learning to read. Use the book band colour your child is reading in school to help you make a good choice. *Hop and Run* is a good choice for children reading at Yellow Band in their classroom to read independently.

The aim of independent reading is to read this book with ease, so that your child enjoys the story and relates it to their own experiences.

About the book

Mouse and Rabbit are playing in the garden. They're having lots of fun hopping and running, Then a plant pot gets broken and they both run away!

Before reading

Help your child to learn how to make good choices by asking: "Why did you choose this book? Why do you think you will enjoy it?" Look at the cover together and ask: "What do you think the story will be about?" Support your child to think of what they already know about the story context. Read the title aloud and ask: "Why might the story be called *Hop and Run*? Who can you see on the cover that will hop? Who can you see that will run?" Remind your child that they can try to sound out the letters to make a word if they get stuck.

Decide together whether your child will read the story independently or read it aloud to you. When books are short, as at Yellow Band, your child may wish to do both!

During reading

If reading aloud, support your child if they hesitate or ask for help by telling the word. Remind your child of what they know and what they can do independently.

If reading to themselves, remind your child that they can come and ask for your help if stuck.

After reading

Support comprehension by asking your child to tell you about the story. Help your child think about the messages in the book that go beyond the story and ask: "Why do you think the boy looked cross? Why do you think Rabbit and Mouse ran away?"

Give your child a chance to respond to the story: "Did you have a favourite part? What would you do if you broke something by accident when you were playing?"

Use the story trail to encourage your child to retell the story in the right sequence, in their own words.

Extending learning

Help your child understand the story structure by using the same sentence patterns and adding some new elements. "Let's make up a new story about Rabbit and Mouse playing somewhere else. In my story they are playing in a school. Rabbit hopped over the table. Mouse ran under the table. Rabbit hopped over the books. Mouse ran under the books. Rabbit hopped over the pencils. Oh no! Rabbit hit the pencils. Now you try. Where will Rabbit and Mouse play in your story?"

Your child's teacher will be talking about punctuation at Yellow Band. On a few of the pages, check your child can recognise capital letters, full stops and exclamation marks by asking them to point these out.

Franklin Watts
First published in Great Britain in 2017
by The Watts Publishing Group

Copyright © The Watts Publishing Group 2017

Series Editors: Jackie Hamley and Melanie Palmer
Series Advisors: Dr Sue Bodman and Glen Franklin
Series Designer: Peter Scoulding

A CIP catalogue record for this book is
available from the British Library.

ISBN 978 1 4451 5465 7 (hbk)
ISBN 978 1 4451 5466 4 (pbk)
ISBN 978 1 4451 6077 1 (library ebook)

Printed in China

Franklin Watts
An imprint of
Hachette Children's Group
Part of The Watts Publishing Group
Carmelite House
50 Victoria Embankment
London EC4Y 0DZ

An Hachette UK Company
www.hachette.co.uk

www.franklinwatts.co.uk